CONTENTS

CHAPTER 1: HER EMERGENCE

In a dark, dark room littered with rotting, dismembered body parts, the cries of the helpless are only ever heard by one twisted, sadistic man. He always cackles gleefully as he tortures, mutilates, and brutalizes his victims. He has cut dozens to pieces over the last twenty years, constantly feeding his vile disorder. The room lays beneath his home, the hatch-door hidden under a tattered rug only a few steps away from his recliner. As he sits in his recliner, he laughs. A stout and balding man. He laughs as he always does, feet kicked up on the coffee table beside the shotgun he has never had to use. He relishes both the pleasure he derives from committing such horrible crimes, and the satisfaction that they always go unpunished. As he leans back in his chair he flips through the channels on his television, just like any other day for him. He sits there chuckling, ignorant to what is transpiring in the damp, dreadful room below. Something not dark or sinister, but almost just.

Past the hatch door and down the stone stairs, the surgical table stands bolted to the floor, blackened by the blood of the dozens he has dragged down again and again over the last two decades. The lone light bulb, dangling over the surgical table, starts to flicker. The blood, pooled on the floor of the terrible room, starts to swirl. It churns and it froths, twisting around the horrible table, a monument to atrocity. From the blood, she arises. A young brown-haired woman. She walks up those stairs and rips open the hatch door, standing defiantly in tattered, bloody clothing.

He sees her, and he panics. He fumbles about, before snatching his shotgun and hastily taking aim. Then she leaps. And he freezes. She descends onto him, knocking him over in his recliner, and he screams.

"Godammit! Godammit! Who are you! Who the fuck are you?"

She strikes him on the nose.

"Godammit! My nose, my fucking nose! You bitch! You stupid fucking bitch!"

She strikes him on the nose again.

"Godammit! Fuck! Shit! You already broke it! You already broke it! What the fuck is wrong with you?"

He reaches for her, trying to snatch her by the neck. She jabs him in the throat and grabs his hand. He hesitates, trying to catch his breath, and she breaks a finger.

"Fuck! Fucking hell! Godammit! I'll kill you! I'll fucking kill you!"

She flips him over, and he tumbles out of his recliner. She pins him on his back and grabs his left arm. She dislocates it from his shoulder.

"Fuck! Fucking hell! You Godamm bitch! Fuck you!"

She then grabs his right arm and dislocates it. He wails and thrashes beneath her. She climbs off his back and leans over him. He looks up at her, glaring, with only hate in his eyes. She flicks him in the eye. And she asks him.

"Where do you keep them?"

He spits on her face. Without even hesitating, she flicks him in the eye again. He grits his teeth.

"Quit flicking me in the Godamm eyeball! Fucking what? Where do I keep what?"

She points at the hatch door. Her gray-blue eyes stare through him with grim determination.

"Where do you keep the things you use in there?"

"Down the hall. Door on the right. You can't fucking miss it." He seethes, itching to kill her, but is immobilized by his dislocated limbs. She walks down the hall and enters the room. Razor-sharp blades and worn-in restraints lay arranged on an old, decaying shelf. She finds many horrible things. A hacksaw, a cattle prod, a cleaver, and a flail. And then she finds the one. A broadsword, mounted on the wall. She takes it, and holds it in her right hand. She clenches the leather hilt as she looks into her reflection off the polished, steel blade. She selects a back-holster off the shelf and sheathes the broadsword, a worthy instrument for her fury.

She opens the closet door across the hall and finds women's clothing. All of it has been meticulously organized, as if it has been filed. She puts on jeans, combat boots, and fingerless gloves. She then dons a black leather jacket with four zippers. As she exits, she opens the first zipper. She walks back into the living room and approaches the horrible, crumpled man. She relocates his right shoulder and then his left. He howls in pain.

"Godammit! What do you want? What's your fucking plan here?"

"I need a ride, bud. You got a car?" she asks.

"It's a truck. I have a pickup truck. Don't you fucking know how to drive?" he snaps back. She bonks him on the head with the flat of her broadsword. And he still remains indignant. "You broke my finger, how the hell do you expect me to drive like this?" He stares at her with venomous hate. And she calmly splints the finger for him.

He looks at his splinted fingers and curses under his breath. He races back to the shotgun, astray on the floor, and aims it at her. She kicks him across the face, knocking him over and kicking the gun aside.

"Quit dawdling and let's get out of this shithole. I've got a lot of work to do." She walks out the door, back turned, confident that he has submitted. He can't let her go off on her own. She's seen his face. She's seen the room. As she strides away, the man makes himself a promise.

"I'm gonna fucking kill this Godamm bitch." In a blind rage he leaves the shotgun behind and follows her compulsively out the door. He unlocks both doors to his rugged, black pickup truck. They each enter, and as he sits behind the wheel with this woman who outsmarted him, who beat him, who humiliated him, he slams his hand down on the dashboard.

"Look, where are we going? What's your plan? What the fuck are you even up to?"

She bonks him on the head with the flat of her broadsword again. "Enough with the questions, buddy. Let's get a move on here."

"There's something I want to get out of the shed first," he tells her.

"Not part of the plan. Make a right out of your driveway. I'll tell you where to turn."

"What are you now, a fucking GPS?" he asks sarcastically.

"Remember what I said about questions, bud?"

"God fucking dammit." He pulls away from his house, and they head down the long and dusty road. She places her broadsword on the dashboard, and they ride in silence for quite some time. They pass by birch trees lined up along the road, bark peeling away like strips of paper. A canopy of bright green leaves hangs over them as they wind down the county highway.

"You got a name?" he asks her.

"Nope, don't got one buddy," she replies.

"My name's Clyde, thanks for asking." He grumbles in annoyance. As they drive further down the road, she looks off to her right and sees a massive, enchanting blue river. Her first real sight of beauty after emerging from such a vile place. They follow the road along the river until they happen upon a small town, where they come across a hardware store.

"We're going to make a quick stop here," she tells him.

"Great, a quick stop, sounds good. Just fucking great," he mutters.

"Gonna need some cash, buddy."

"Fucking hell! In the glovebox, in the fucking glovebox!" Clyde yells. "There's a shitload of money in there. I was saving it in case... I guess it doesn't matter anymore, huh? Just fucking take it," he groans. She opens the glovebox and finds a bundle of $100 bills, which she pockets. She exits the truck and walks into the old, dusty hardware store. The man behind the counter greets her.

"Welcome to Advantage Hardware, ma'am! Do you need help finding anything?"

"I know exactly what I need," she replies. She walks up and down the aisles, gathering the tools she needs to enact her plan. She buys three things. A pair of pliers, a book of matches, and a packet of borax. She places them in the zippers of her jacket and returns back to the truck.

"What, did you even buy anything?" Clyde asks.

"Questions, Clyde. Remember what happens when you ask questions?"

"Fucking hell, where to now?" he whines.

"Keep driving down the road and I'll tell you where to stop, bud."

They pull out of the shopping center and continue down the road. And Clyde sits there seething. He's angry. He's resentful. He hates her. He can't believe it. After all these years, all these years, he's been caught. He thought he'd never have to pay. This man, this twisted man, who came from a broken home. A mother he never knew. A father who beat him, and didn't care if Clyde beat others. Didn't care if he tortured others. Didn't care if he killed others. First bugs. Then birds. Then cats. Then women. This man, this twisted man takes so much pleasure from it. And he can't help himself. He pulls a knife out of the center console and swings it at her. She grabs his wrist, and twists it.

"Godammit! God fucking dammit!" He nearly careens off the road, but slams on the brakes and the truck comes to a stop. She breaks another finger. "Shit! Fucking shit!" he screams. "Seriously, you want me to keep fucking driving you like this?"

"I'm not splinting that one for you," she tells him. "Learn to live with it, bud."

"Godammit, fucking hell..." he grumbles. "Is this it? This is how it's gonna be? You understand the kind of fucking person I am, don't you?"

"Oh, you bet I understand you," she tells him.

"You should smile more. All throughout this bullshit you've just had that same, ugly, determined fucking look on your face. It's unnerving."

"Quit whining, and quit wasting my time," she tells him.

"Godammit, so down the road? Keep going down this

fucking road?"

"Yup, that's the plan," she says.

"Fuckin' shit." He pulls back onto the road and continues to drive, furious at the woman sitting next to him. They merge onto a highway and sit in silence as the hours go by. She watches as other cars move between lanes, and as traffic slows and starts as they carry along. She sees such a crowded world. They pull off the highway as the sun begins to set, and Clyde begins to grow even more impatient.

"So, Lady No-Name, what's your plan here? It's getting late. We're almost out of gas."

"Well good thing there's a gas station coming up, bud," she replies.

"Gas station, fucking… can't even fucking….'" he mutters.

"What's bugging you now?" she asks.

"You are! You fucking bitch! What are we even doing? Is this some game to you? What's your fucking problem? Godammit! You broke my fingers, my nose, every part of my body hurts! And I've been driving your ass around for how long? I can't take it! I'm tired, I'm starving… Godamm I'm fucking hungry."

"They've got food at gas stations," she tells him.

"Gas station food? Seriously? I'm not eating that fucking garbage."

"Well, what do you like to eat?" she asks.

"I… I like barbecue," he answers.

"Barbecue? On my dollar? I don't think so, Clyde."

"Fucking… whatever. Godammit. So be it," he mumbles. They pull into the gas station, and Clyde begins to exit the truck.

"Where do you think you're going, bud?" she asks him.

"I'm getting out to pump the fucking gas."

"I can pump the gas, Clyde. Wait in the truck," she tells him.

"Godammit, fucking... get me a ham and cheese or something."

She exits the truck and walks into the gas station market. A cluttered assortment of junk-food and cheap toiletries line the store under a ray of fluorescent light. The light reflects off her leather jacket as she heads toward the beverage aisle, looking downward at her first objective. A drain in the floor, meant for cleaning spills. Shuddering at the sight of it, she opens the second zipper and removes the packet of borax. She tears open the packet and dumps it down the drain, before closing the second zipper and turning away from it. Her body relaxes as she grabs two bottles of water off the shelf and two sandwiches. A young Cajun French man greets her as she approaches the register, wearing an orange employee vest and a black baseball cap.

"You find everything you need today, ma'am?" he asks.

"Yes, I did." She looks at his nametag. "Randall. Can I also get $80 on 3, please?"

"Absolutely," he answers. "This your first time in Louisiana?"

"Yes, it is," she replies.

"Where are you coming from?" he asks. She pauses for a moment to think.

"Mississippi. South of Jackson," she answers.

"What brings you down here to Henderson?"

"Just... just seeing the sights," she says.

"Well, there are lots of great sights to see in Henderson, ma'am. You should take an airboat ride through the bayou. Lots of people love to do that and see the gators. But there's a lot of great food around here too. Tell me, have you ever eaten jambalaya?"

"No, I haven't. What is it?" she asks.

"Oh, it has a little bit of everything, ma'am. Rice, sausage, chicken, shrimp, and lots of veggies. Me and my mom eat it at home all the time. But if you end up passing through Breaux Bridge, there's a great little diner there that serves it."

"What's the name of this place?" she asks.

"It's called Cyril's Creole Diner. Even though we eat it at home all the time, there's something special about grabbing a bowl at Cyril's."

"Good to know, Randall. Thank you for your help today." She collects her things and exits the store. She hands Clyde the water and sandwiches.

"Egg Salad? Seriously? Who knows how long this shit has been sitting out?" Clyde whines. He unwraps the sandwich as she starts pumping the gas.

"We're stopping at a motel for the night," she tells him. "You take the bed. I'll take the couch. I want to stay by the television. There's a story on the news that I want to keep my eye on."

"Not gonna complain about that," he answers. But then he pauses. "And I suppose that way you can stay between me and the door. I know every trick in the book, Lady No-Name. This won't end well for you. You'll be sorry you fucking messed with me! Whatever this is, whatever mind game you're playing, it'll be the end of you. You should have run away when you had the chance!" He chuckles to himself. "I won't hesitate, bitch. We both know I'm not your prisoner. I just can't let you run off on your own. Loose ends, and all that. Can't have 'em."

"Can it, Clyde. You talk too much." She finishes pumping the gas and steps back into the truck. They pull out of the gas station, Clyde muttering to himself as she gazes out the window. There's so much for her to do. So much for her to fix. So much cruelty in this world. And yet there is kindness. She watches as a man helps an elderly woman across the road, as couples hold hands, and as children play and laugh.

She knows how cruelty hides everywhere. How sinister things lurk anywhere. How malevolence takes root, takes hold, and takes over. How even in a small, quaint town like this one, evil can slither its way in. As they approach the motel, she looks away from the window and sighs. Then as they pull into the motel parking lot, they hear a loud thump.

"Godammit! Fuck!" Clyde yells.

"What is it now?" she asks.

"That's a puncture, we've got a fucking flat tire," he answers.

"You've got a spare, don't you?"

"Yeah I do… but…" he trails off, and looks away from her.

"What's the matter, don't you know how to change a tire?"

"Fuck you! Of course I do. I'll take care of it." They exit the truck, and she holsters the broadsword with just her right hand. Clyde stands in the parking lot, and he looks at his hand. With his two broken fingers. He grits his teeth. "Fuckin' bitch."

CHAPTER 2:
SOB STORY

Randall stands outside the gas station market, holding his lit cigarette in his hand. He looks across the road, eyes fixed on the lush, green field across the way. He watches a gray-feathered heron bob its head back and forth, as it paces through the grass. He takes a drag from his cigarette, and holds the smoke in his lungs as he watches the bird strut through the field. Randall sees this bird every day, and he always wonders what it is doing away from its flock. As he slowly exhales the smoke, the bird flaps its wings and flies away. He takes one last drag from his cigarette, before ashing it in the tray atop the rubbish bin outside the market. He sighs and walks back into the market. His elderly coworker, Gertie, stands behind the counter as he puts his employee vest back on.

"You all done with your smoke break, Randall?" Gertie asks.

"All done for now, Gertie," he replies. "What do you reckon that heron is doing over in that field every day? It seems awfully strange to see one apart from its flock."

"You and that bird, Randall Foret." Gertie chuckles. "I think you like that bird, Randall, because it's there for you every day. A little bit of routine and entertainment makes things more interesting."

"I suppose you're right, Gertie. Things can get slow around here, after all."

"Can you go ahead and face aisle three? It's looking awfully cluttered over there."

"Sure thing, Gertie." Randall replies. He walks over to the aisle, beginning to face the products. Before he can even start, the market door chimes and a large, unkempt man enters the store. He twitches and scratches the inside of his arm, before approaching Gertie at the register.

"I'll take a pack of Sphinx Menthol Shorts."

"Sorry honey, we're all out of those today," Gertie replies. "Is there another brand you'd like to buy?"

"I come in and buy those cigarettes every day!" The man furrows his brow and puts his hand on the countertop. "You're out?"

"Yes, I'm sorry sir. We should have them back in stock on Tuesday," Gertie tells him. The man scratches his arm again and leans forward over the countertop, looking Gertie straight in the eyes.

"Maybe I should just take what I want then, you old hag!" He reaches over the counter, snarling at Gertie as she pulls away from him. Randall knocks over a bottle of vinegar in the confusion, and he rushes over to the counter as the bottle smashes on the floor. Randall shoves the man away from Gertie, screaming at the top of his lungs.

"Get the fuck out! Get the fuck out or we're calling the cops! Out! Now!" The man turns and hobbles out of the store, staring at Randall with a look of both anger and pain. Randall turns to Gertie and rushes over to the counter.

"Gertie! Are you okay? That was insane! What that man did was completely out of line!"

"Randall, that man was Louis. You know him, he's a local sob story. He wasn't in the right mind. Don't worry about it, honey," Gertie answers.

"Gertie, I can't understand how you put up with people like that."

"Well, now that it's over Randall, could you be a dear and mop up that vinegar? Just push it into the drain. That's what it's there for," Gertie asks. Randall goes behind the counter and grabs the mop and bucket, and pushes the spilt vinegar into the drain in the floor. A shudder runs down his spine. He then grabs a dustpan to collect the broken glass.

"It's always something around here, Gertie," Randall sighs.

Gertie looks up at Randall from behind the counter. "You know Randall, you're a young guy. You're only 22. You could still go to college, and have a career. You have your whole life ahead of you."

Randall chuckles as he discards the broken glass. "Gertie, I know it can get chaotic here, but I like it. I like my job. You don't have to worry about me." Randall continues about his tasks as the hours go by, toiling away as cars pull in and customers walk in and out. Whenever Randall gets annoyed with his job, he pushes those thoughts to the back of his head, and just focuses on the task right in front of him. He doesn't want to think about all the other places he could be. He doesn't want to think about the community college in Lafayette, that he has been told again and again to enroll at. Randall isn't ready to move on. He remains in the comfort of his small town, working away at the gas station without a clear goal in sight. He continues stocking the shelves and sweeping the floor until his shift draws near to an end.

"Well Gertie, it's about that time. I suppose I should start heading on home."

"Alright then Randall, you have a good rest of your day," Gertie replies. "Say hello to your mother for me."

Randall puts on his backpack and heads down Henderson Road, passing by the thrift shops and bars that line the street along the way. As he walks further he looks off into the bayou, gazing at the cypress trees standing in the water. He usually sees a large number of gators lining the bayou waters, but today they are only sparse, and he sees three of them swimming away as he walks down the road.

As he approaches his home, he takes a sigh of relief before entering the door. His mother Zoe stands behind the kitchen counter, chopping carrots for the night's dinner. The television plays the local news in the background.

"Welcome home, sweetie," she tells him. "How was work?"

"Oh the usual Mom. Although there was some excitement today. Had to chase Louis out of the store."

"Oh, that Louis," Zoe sighs. "I pray for that man. One day that meth is going to kill him."

"What's on the TV?" Randall asks.

"Oh, just more on that corruption scandal, with that city councilman in Houston," she replies.

"John Carver? I can't believe he keeps getting reelected. You have to wonder what they're even thinking down there." He pauses as he looks away from the television. "That Louis though. I just feel terrible for him. There should be a way for that man to get help. It's atrocious. He roams around this town, barely scraping by. As far as I'm concerned, Louis is afflicted. And we just let people like him rot."

"Randall, sweetie, you just said you had to chase him away today!" Zoe exclaims.

"Why would you suddenly feel like that?"

Randall sighs and sets down his backpack. "I didn't even recognize him today, Mom. I've seen him all over town. And today, he just seemed like a completely different person. It's just so wrong. The man is spiraling, and there's nothing he can do about it. He's helpless, Mom."

"Randall, you've always been an empathetic person. But you have no way of knowing what that man is really going through. You should spend more time focusing on yourself. You could still go to college, you know."

Randall groans and removes his pack of cigarettes from his shirt pocket. Zoe turns and looks at Randall disheartenedly. "You should really quit those things, Randall. I don't know why you keep smoking. It'll kill you, sweetie. And you're smart enough to know that."

"You just don't get it Mom. Why I use these." He puts a cigarette in his mouth and heads toward the back door of their home. "It's to turn down the noise. Something you don't need yourself." Randall exits the back door and sits down on the porch outside. He lights his cigarette and looks into the stream that runs past their home. He takes a long drag from his cigarette. As he looks into the stream, he sees the crawfish scattering away, evacuating the waters and scuttering into the brush. He stands up in surprise. "Something's going on with the wildlife here..." he mutters, as he takes another drag.

CHAPTER 3: PHOBIA

"Councilman Carver! Watchdog groups have accused you of accepting bribes from Mason Industries in exchange for silencing whistleblowers and burying evidence that exposes the firm's use of substandard materials in the construction of the Hibiscus Park Affordable Housing Development. How do you respond to these allegations?"

John Carver straightens his red tie as he stares into the camera, smirking at the reporter as she points her microphone toward him. "The accusations of collusion between myself and Mason Industries are completely false. They are fabricated attempts at discrediting the Hibiscus Park development, which is being constructed to ensure that citizens of Houston have access to quality housing regardless of their financial circumstances. Hibiscus Park is being built to help the blue-collar families of Houston, expand their quality of life, and keep Texas great. No further comment."

John turns away from the reporter, walking back toward

his office in the confines of Houston City Hall. What a fuck up. What an enormous, catastrophic turn of events. His own greed and collusion caught, all by one damn whistleblower. He'd love to know who it was, and kill them himself. So what if he treats his position of City Councilman like a racket? Who wouldn't cut corners for a little extra cash? But the press, they drone around like gnats. Vermin that sniffed out his corruption. How he despises them. He ponders about what America would be like, without them buzzing around.

His staff members wait for him, lingering outside his small, cluttered office. They look at him nervously, reeling back just from the look of malice in his eyes.

"I'm getting the hell out of here," he tells them. He looks around the room, grumbling in annoyance at his panicked staff. "I'm going back to the private office. Have Eddie get the car ready. Where the fuck is my umbrella?"

His intern Danny looks up from his phone. "Sir, there's not a cloud in the sky out there. I'll have Eddie pull the car around, but I think you'll be fine without your umbrella."

John grimaces at Danny, clenching his fist and looking him straight in the eye. "My phobia! You imbecile! My fucking phobia! Who the hell hired this dumbass?" He walks up to Danny as his staff members scramble, rifling through his office in search of his umbrella. "You work for me? Me! John Carver! And you give me lip about my fucking umbrella. It's not funny you moron! Get the hell out of my face. You're fucking fired." Danny rushes away from John as his assistant Jacqueline hands him his umbrella.

"I'm very sorry about that sir! He's terminated, we'll make sure you won't see him again." Jacqueline smiles at him, running her hands nervously through her long blonde hair as she gazes into his weary, blue eyes.

"Thank you, Jacqueline." John opens his pitch-black umbrella as he walks past her. "Make sure you come back to the private office as well. We'll be working overtime trying to clear up this clusterfuck." John exits out the back of city hall, holding his umbrella over his head as the sun beats down on the pavement in the parking lot, a black SUV with tinted windows waiting idle for him. He enters the back of the car, his driver Eddie ready behind the wheel.

"You're having quite the day, aren't you sir?" Eddie pulls away as John relaxes in the back of the car.

"Eddie, you know I fucking hate this. This life. I'm not meant for it. Working from dawn till dusk. Dealing with all these fucking morons, every day. The press, they're like vultures."

Eddie sighs as he taps his fingers on the steering wheel. "Sir, you know that you're meant for this. It's in your blood. I know it's difficult at times. But you're better than these other people you surround yourself with. I know they test you sir. And I know the media, they irritate you. But you can do so much more. City Council today, John. But you know we're not stopping there."

John smirks over at Eddie and runs his hand through his thick gray hair. "That Jacqueline, Eddie. What do you think about her? I was thinking maybe I'll take her home one of these days. She's got spunk, that one."

Eddie laughs as he fiddles with his sunglasses. "I know you've always had a thing for blondes, sir. I say do it. You could use the distraction."

John smiles as he gazes out the window. "Eddie, I think you're right. It's just about time with her. She's almost ready."

Eddie chuckles as he pulls the SUV into the office parking lot. John exits the vehicle, opening the black umbrella before stepping out onto the pavement. He walks into the office, the eyes of his employees averting as he strolls down the hall.

Manila files lay scattered around the office as his subordinates dash between their cubicles, desperately answering the phones as they try to persuade callers that no scandal has taken place. John walks past his panicking staff and sits down in his office, the blinds shuttered and the room dimly lit by a single lamp.

John leans back in his leather chair, fingers tapping on his mahogany desk as he grinds his teeth and puts his hand on his forehead. He tenses up every time he hears the phones ring, his head throbbing and his hands shaking as he leans over the table.

"Jacqueline! In here! Now!" John bangs his clenched fist on the desk. Jacqueline hurries into his office, her hands meekly at her side as John scowls at her unnervingly. "Jacqueline! Where's my cocaine? You know I can't make it through the day without it! Get it in here! Now!"

"Right… right away, sir." Jacqueline hurries out of the office as John opens his desk drawer, frantically rummaging through the drawers of his desk until he finds his metal straw hidden beneath the clutter. He lets out a sigh of relief as Jacqueline comes back into his office, presenting him with a pile of cocaine on a glass tray, as well as a razor blade.

"Fucking… finally Jacqueline. Thank you." John picks up the razor blade and starts cutting lines of the cocaine as Jacqueline lingers in his office.

"Of course sir. Whatever you need, I'm here." Jacqueline walks away as John snorts a line of cocaine off the tray, his headache easing as his hands stop shaking. He sets down his straw and loosens up in his chair, massaging his forehead before the phone on his desk starts to ring. John picks up the phone, muttering under his desk as his secretary answers.

"Sir, there's Matt Bowen from Mason Industries on line 1 for you. Do you want me to put him through?"

"Go ahead, put the jackass through," John groans. He snorts another line of cocaine as the phone beeps. "Go for Carver."

"Carver! You asshole! You unbelievable fucking asshole!

How could you have possibly screwed this up? You're supposed to be a Godamm professional! I should have never worked with your kind!"

"Just fuck off, Bowen. It's over. This Godamm little trick we tried to pull is over. I could care less. You know, life has its ups and downs. And for me, I'll be back on my feet in no time. You, on the other hand, probably knee deep quaking in your own shit, huh? My constituents, they'll keep voting for me. This is just a little setback. But you Matt, I bet you're fucked, huh?"

"Carver, if I ever see you again you're dead. Fucking dead! This shouldn't have been hard to pull off. If you weren't so coked out all the time you could've handled this! And now I'm stuck here at headquarters in fucking Dallas, my own board ready to tear me limb from limb. As if they could."

John snickers as he rolls his metal straw between his fingers. "I'm not scared of you in the slightest, Bowen. You're fucked. I'm not. So quit fucking calling. I can't believe you ever talked me into it. I should have known better than to work with scum like you."

"Dead, Carver. You're fucking dead!" The line disconnects, and John lets out an exasperated sigh as he snorts another line. With each day that passes for him, he grows more and more weary. He continues to sit at his desk, snorting cocaine and pacing about until the sun starts setting. More and more, as the days pass for John, the whining, the phones, and the constant campaigning does nothing but drive him further and further disturbed. Only rarely does he have the opportunity to fill the void in him, to set only a temporary correction for the misery of a man who wants nothing more than to binge day in and day out.

Dark desires, a distraction he wants nothing more than. A chance to feel powerful, an adrenaline rush that can't be matched by simple, squalid habits like cocaine. John Carver marches to his work and back every day, even the allure of being a politician inconsequential to him in comparison. After years of accomplishing so little, he thought that politics might lead him toward a path of power. But John still can't change the man he is. A man fueled by his own baseline urges, trying to fill a role in society he was never meant to.

After the sunlight fades, John gathers his things and leaves the office, entering the back of his SUV that waits for him in the parking lot. As Eddie pulls away, John gazes through the tinted window with his bloodshot eyes. He watches as the other cars pass by, and as the brightly lit open signs on businesses fade out. John mutters under his breath as the streetlights begin to turn on.

"I fucking hate this, Eddie. You're sure? You're sure this will lead to more? I'm a city councilman! A fucking councilman! How much longer do I have to put myself through this?"

Eddie sighs as he pulls off the main road and toward John's neighborhood. "Sir, the wait will be inconsequential compared to what your reward will be. You could shape this country into paradise. Paradise, for people like you."

The security guard tips his hat as they drive through the large, metal gate outside John's neighborhood. Eddie pulls onto John's estate, and turns around in his seat to look John in the eyes.
"Ups and downs, John. Ups and downs. Like it always has been. Make sure to get some sleep tonight. You'll have a long day ahead of you tomorrow."

John sighs as he exits the car. "Thank you for everything today, Eddie. I'll see you in the morning." John enters his estate and walks into his study, pacing around as he tries to burn off his extra energy. He sits down in his chair and takes a long, deep sigh. He's running himself ragged, desperately trying to cling to a seat of power that seems so irrelevant in the moment. City Councilman. What a joke. But long term, it could lead to immeasurable change. Real change. For Carver, the time it will take is inconsequential. But the fatigue, the drama, the constant whining, it still takes its toll. But so what of the wait? It won't be so long, not really. Even so, the days couldn't go by slower. For every person that John has to work with, he feels nothing but loathing.

Before long he sighs and heads for his bedroom. He putters about, muttering to himself before he collapses over the sheets. He tosses and turns, his eyes dry and his mouth sore from a long day of grinding his teeth. As John's weary eyes close shut, he lets out a drowsy groan of indignation.

"I fucking hate it! I hate sleeping all night."

CHAPTER 4:
BRAIN FOG

"That Bastard! That Godamm fucking bastard!" Matt paces around his executive office, clutching a bottle of whiskey. "I'll kill him! I'll fucking kill him!" He takes a swig from the bottle and walks toward the ceiling-high glass panes that normally give him a full view of Dallas, running his hand through his slick blonde hair. In recent weeks, that view has been obscured by a thick, white fog, an unusual phenomenon for the city. He looks into the fog, his hand trembling as he clutches the bottle. That fucking idiot. John Carver, a slimeball he should have never picked up the phone for. His kind, they don't have a sense of morals, nor foresight. All seems meaningless to men like John Carver, who find no act of crime or collusion to be of much consequence. To Matt, every screwup like this only serves to drive him down further.

He takes another swig and continues pacing around the

room. He puts his hand against the wall, leaning over and trying to support his body. He takes a deep breath and staggers out of his office, onto the main floor. He approaches his secretary, Leah. "Leah! Leah! Has she called? Please tell me she's called. I need her now more than ever."

Leah sighs and turns toward Matt with a somber look on her face. "I'm sorry sir, she still hasn't called." She brushes aside her curly, black hair and looks away from him.

Matt groans and staggers back to his office. "Emma... I need Emma. She thinks I'm a monster. She doesn't understand at all."

Leah sits at her desk and rests her hand on her forehead. "Matthew Bowen... I don't know how much more of you I can take," she mutters. She gets up from her seat and heads toward the coffee maker, where the floor manager, Bill, stands drinking coffee from a styrofoam cup.

"Don't tell me the bastard's drunk again," he quips, taking a sip of his coffee.

"I can't stand working for the man. It's one breakdown after another with him. And all this overtime, it's already dark and we're still here. It's as if he doesn't want to go back home alone. The man's so high maintenance."

"He's not going to make it much longer," Bill sighs. "He just wasn't cut out for this. It was his father, left him as CEO, you know. And all that shit with his wife. I can't even blame her."
"So you don't think it'll be much longer, Bill?"

"He's on his way out," Bill says. "We won't have to put up with him much longer." Bill sighs and finishes his coffee, before tossing the styrofoam cup in the rubbish bin. "He's consistently fucked up, unimagineably."

"That would be best for everyone here, I think," Leah replies. She fills her own cup of coffee as Bill leans against the counter. "What do you think about all this fog, Bill? Pretty freaky, especially for Dallas."

"Oh, it's a complete clusterfuck," Bill replies. "I can hardly make it to work every morning. You can't see four feet in front of you, driving over here." Bill leans back off the counter and back onto his feet. "We should both get back to work. No sense in angering him further." Bill walks back to his own office, as Leah finishes sipping on her coffee and returns to her desk.

Matt approaches Leah as she sits back down. "Leah, I'm sorry. For how I've been acting. It's just one thing after another. I can't take it. I'm glad you're still here, working with me."

Leah looks up at Matt and sighs. "I'm sure you'll get through it sir. Everyone has their own ups and downs."

Matt sighs in relief. "Thank you, Leah." He returns back to his executive office, and picks up a picture of his wife, standing on his desk. She has black hair and blue eyes, and Matt stares into them, with a look of longing. "I need you, Emma. Please come back." He grabs his bottle of whiskey off his desk and walks toward the window panes, gazing into the thick white fog, looming over the city of Dallas.

The drinking, bottle after bottle. It does nothing but drive him further and further down, spiraling at high speed into his own miserable design. He resents his father, the man who never gave time for him. The man who never saw Matt as more than a successor. Forced into boarding schools, he hardly ever saw his father face to face. And his mother, distant and aloof, outsourcing his care to the nanny. Matt feels nothing but bitterness for his family, and blames everyone but himself for the mess he finds himself in. As he gazes into the fog, the irony is lost on him. Just like the liquor, it keeps him from changing.

Matt takes another swig of his whiskey as he walks out of his office, and down the hall. The night guard, Owen, looks up as Matt leans on the wall. "Another rough night, sir?"

"It's always something, Owen. Always fucking something."

"You can't make all that disappear with a bottle of whiskey, sir. You're an alcoholic. I'm one as well. But I'm in recovery. Three years sober, not even a drop. There's a meeting every night only a couple blocks from here. You could go with me, sir. It's never too late to change."

Matt sighs as he takes another swig. "You know Owen, I wouldn't let anyone else here talk to me like that. And if you haven't had a drop in three years, then how are you still an alcoholic?"

"Alcoholism is a disease, Matt. You can stop drinking, but you'll never stop being an alcoholic. If I had even a drop right now, I'd be right back where I started." Owen chuckles in self-contemplation. "It won't stop until you accept that."

Matt groans as he takes another swig and walks past Owen. "I'm in full control of my drinking, Owen. Those meetings are batshit. Might have worked for you. But I'm too smart for them."

"It's not that you're too smart for them. Or that they only work on the more simple-minded. You have to humble yourself if you want to enter recovery. You don't have to overthink everything."

Matt pushes the button on the elevator as he looks back at Owen. "Thanks for the advice, Owen. I don't intend to take it." He enters the elevator, still clutching the bottle in his hand. As he descends toward the bottom floor, he sees his distorted reflection off the metal elevator door. The eyes that stare back at him look nothing like the man he used to be. He looks away, and takes another swig.

As the elevator door opens, Matt staggers over to the back of the building, where his driver waits idle in his limo. Matt immediately presses the button to raise the privacy window between him and his driver, and lurches back in his seat as they drive through the fog. Just like the fog looming over the city, Matt sedates his mind until he finds himself lost in a gloomy haze. The feeling he chases, after having to go so long without her.

His wife, his work, his own well-being. All things that Matt sabotages over and over again. A man trapped by his own urges. He throws everything away just to feel that feeling, the same one that has brought him so much comfort. He would like to say it does the trick every time. But every time Matt drinks, he loses his bliss little by little. As his driver pulls onto his estate, Matt staggers out of his limo and mutters under his breath.

"This Godamm fog… and at this time."

CHAPTER 5: WHAT MAKES A MONSTER

"Took you all day to fix that flat, huh Clyde?" She looks out the window of the truck, gazing into the night sky. She basks in the glow of the moon and the shine of the stars. She wants to see more. But she can't let herself grow distracted. "I thought you said you knew how to change a tire."

"Two broken fingers! Two Godammit! This coming from the bitch who can't even drive her own ass around." Clyde hunches over the steering wheel, twitching with agitation. "It's already night! I've been busting my balls all day, and now we're on this fucking road again. You mind telling me where the fuck we're going?"

She reluctantly looks away from the stars to turn back to Clyde, who is a far less pretty sight. "Again with that question, Clyde? You should focus more on the road in front of you. If you had done that yesterday, we could've been there already."

Clyde rolls his eyes. "As far as I can tell, you're fucking crazy, Lady No-Name. So what place is so important that you need me, a fucking killer, to be your Godamm chauffeur?"

She looks Clyde dead in the eyes. She doesn't trust him. But she can handle him. "Houston, Clyde. We're going to Houston. That's our first stop, anyway." Clyde becomes even more annoyed, and lets out a loud, indignant sigh.

"First stop, huh? How many are we going to fucking make?" he groans.

"We'll see how you do in Houston, bud," she answers. "But since you're always complaining about being hungry, we are going to stop for dinner." His ears perk up.

"And where will that be?" he asks. They approach a bridge with a large sign towering over it. *Welcome to Breaux Bridge - Crawfish Capital of the World.* The water beneath them shimmers in the moonlight as they drive over the bridge. They drive through the town, passing old brick buildings and storefronts. The streets are alive, with bar hoppers and sightseers strolling along downtown. They approach a diner with an old, well-worn sign. *Cyril's Creole Diner.*

"We're stopping here," she tells him.

"Oh, c'mon, a diner? This place looks like a shithole," Clyde whines.

"Don't push your luck, bud."

They pull into the parking lot and walk into the diner. It is a simple place, housed in a brick building. Inside are wooden tables, old booths, and checkered tablecloths. Only a handful of people eat inside, conversing peacefully as they eat their food. An African-American woman greets them.

"Welcome to Cyril's! My name is Marie, I'll be your waitress this evening." She sits them down in a booth and hands them their menus. "I'll be right back to take your order, okay?" She walks

29

away, and Clyde takes a look around himself.

"See? Fuckin' shithole. I called it. This place is dirty, run down, hell this booth is filthy!" He looks at his menu. "And look, there's all this weird local shit on here. Why the fuck did we have to stop here of all places?"

"I've heard good things about it," she replies.

"From fucking who?" he snaps. But then he grins widely. "Don't tell me you made a friend, Lady No-Name..?"

"And what would you care?" she snaps back. But Clyde stares right through her, baring his crooked teeth.

"People like us, lady, people like us. We can't make friends. They always rat. Or they end up dead. And you should hope for the latter." He grits his teeth. "People like us, people like us who love, just love to hurt. And maim. And bruise, and cut and slash. We can't just make friends. I'm guessing whoever told you about this place was some fucking normie. If he really knew you, knew about this, knew about who you're with, and what you're doing right now, he would be terrified." He continues to posture, menacing over the checkered tablecloth. But then she chuckles.

"Us? You mean you and me?" She laughs out loud. "Clyde, buddy, we're not the same. We're not the same kind of people. And I'm not keeping you around to be my friend..." She smirks at him, as if he were a child. "If that's where you're going with this, bud."

His face sours. "I know we're not friends, you bitch. And as soon as you drop your guard, as soon as you get comfortable, you're dead! And I'll enjoy it. It'll be an all-timer for me. I'm looking forward to it."

"Whatever gets you up in the morning," she replies. The waitress walks back over to their table, oblivious to the conversation at hand.

"Are you two ready to order?" the waitress asks.

"Yes, we are," she answers. "Could I have the jambalaya, please?"

"And what would you like to drink with that?"

"What do you normally drink?" she asks.

"Well, ma'am, I personally really like the sweet tea here. We brew it in house."

"I'll have a sweet tea then. That sounds nice. Thank you," she replies. Clyde grimaces over at the waitress.

"I'll take a cheeseburger and fries. And a root beer," Clyde tells her.

"Okay then folks, I'll be right back with your food." The waitress gathers their menus and walks away. Clyde looks back across the table, at her.

"You know, I could teach you a few things, Lady No-Name. About really being savage. About really inflicting pain. About really being terrifying." He raises a chilling smile.

"Oh, do tell, Clyde," she replies. "Because I'm not scared of you in the slightest."

"That's step one!" he laughs. "You don't show fear. That's perfect. Even right now you're staring at me, with that cold, determined look on your face! But that look, it's not terrifying. Not really. Because I can tell you care. You care about others. You care about me, in a way. You don't like me, no. You hate me. You despise me. In that way, you care. You have a sense of principles. Of morality. And that makes you human. Even though you've beaten my ass, and broken my bones... I'm not your hostage! That's why I'm not scared of you!" He laughs, shaking his head in indignation. "Because you're only human."

She stares into him. She doesn't smile. She doesn't smirk, she doesn't frown, she doesn't scowl. She just looks into him. With that same, driven expression. "You know what I think, Clyde?

You think you're more than human. You think you're a monster. You think the fact you truly don't care about others, about consequences, about life, that it makes you superior. More than human. But buddy, it's the opposite. It doesn't mean you're not human. It just makes you vile. It makes you a spoiled brat. It just makes you sick."

The waitress returns back to the table with their food. "Jambalaya for the lady, and a cheeseburger and fries for you, sir. Let me know if you two need anything."

"Thank you very much," she replies. "It looks delicious." The waitress walks away as Clyde cracks open his root beer.

"Godamm, at least I'm finally getting some actual food in me." He looks across the table, at her. "We're not finished with this conversation, Lady No-Name."

"Shut up and eat your cheeseburger, Clyde." She looks into her bowl of jambalaya, and sees an array of colors staring back at her. Green bell peppers, red tomatoes, okra, sausage, shrimp, and chicken, all mixed together in rice. A vibrant mix of reds and greens, and a dash of yellow from the creole seasoning. She picks up her fork and slowly takes a bite of the food. And she smiles. Happy to experience something wholesome. Something real. Something simple. And she appreciates it. In this moment she allows herself to focus on just her meal, and nothing else. Until Clyde gives her an ugly look from across the table.

"What the fuck are you smiling about?" he mumbles. He takes a swig from his root beer and crams a handful of french fries in his mouth. Then he slams his hand down on the table. "Hey, waitress! Idiot! Come back over here!" The waitress reluctantly returns back to the table.

"What seems to be the problem, sir?"

"My fries, that's what! They're fucking cold! What kind of place are you running here? I ought to fucking..." he trails off, as his eyes meet with hers, from across the table, staring into him like daggers.

"Sir, I can... I can take them back if you want," the waitress stammers.

"Just... just fuck off." Clyde seethes, holding in his anger. The waitress hurries away as Clyde shudders in annoyance. From across the table, she lets out a sigh.

"You gonna have a meltdown every time we go out?" she asks. Clyde hunches over the table, breaking eye contact with her.

"I'm just waiting... waiting for that moment you drop your guard." He looks back up at her, with that same chilling smile. "It'll be so much fun, Lady No-Name. When you finally get yours." He laughs, and takes another swig of his root beer. "I haven't felt this excited in years!"

She puts down her fork. "Enjoy the rest of your meal, Clyde. I've got something I should be taking care of. Make sure you behave yourself. I'll be back later." She walks past him and exits the restaurant. And Clyde looks around himself, baffled. He knows he hasn't seen the last of her. But what a mistake. What an enormous blunder. Now that she's not watching, he can have all the fun he wants. He laughs to himself, chuckling gleefully, as he continues eating his meal. Maybe this night won't be such a disappointment after all.

He watches the restaurant's patrons as they chat and eat their food. So oblivious. So completely, utterly oblivious of him. They have no idea just how dangerous and twisted he is. He relaxes in the booth, smiling as looks around. This is the part he loves most. The part where he decides. The part where he chooses which ones live, and the one that dies. It doesn't take long for her to catch his eye.

He watches as Marie, their waitress, gathers her things and throws her purse over her shoulder. Clyde follows her as she exits the restaurant. She turns a corner around the building, and Clyde raises his chilling smile. His hands shake with excitement.

His breathing becomes rapid. He picks up his pace, and turns the corner around the restaurant. But then he freezes. There she is, waiting for him in her black leather jacket.

She kicks Clyde in the groin.

"Fuck! Godammit!" He falls to his knees in pain.

She knees Clyde in the head, knocking him onto his back.

"You bitch! You're dead! You're fucking dead!"

She stands there kicking him, over and over in his ribs.

"Stop it, you bitch! You Godamm fucking bitch!

She then plants her boot down on his chest. And she roars.

"Look at me! Look me in the eyes!" she screams. Clyde squirms, shaking his head, looking anywhere but there. Anywhere but those eyes. She plants her boot down harder.

"C'mon! Look at me, bud! Fucking look at me!"

He can feel the pressure on his chest. And he looks up at her. There she is, staring into him with that same cold, determined expression. It's then he realizes what's really in her gray-blue eyes. Fearlessness, fury, retribution, and most terrifying of all an animosity like he has never seen. He struggles to breathe, not only because of the boot on his chest, but from the terror he feels. A kind of terror that he thought only he could give to people. She takes her boot off his chest, but keeps staring into him. He slowly picks himself up off the ground.

"Godamm, lady. Godammit!" He hunches over in pain. "You'll regret this! You fucking bitch!" He hobbles away from her, heading back toward the pickup truck. She follows him back over and slams his head on the hood of the truck.

"Where do you think you're going? Huh?" She grabs onto his shirt collar and yanks him toward her. "Remember these eyes, Clyde! Remember them! You don't go anywhere unless I say so! You don't fucking breathe unless I say so! And so help me, if you try anything, anything like that again I will fucking end you! You are not the one in control! Not anymore!" She pushes him away as she lets go of his shirt collar. "Now get back in the truck. We have a long night ahead of us."

He gives in, muttering to himself as he unlocks both doors to his truck. They both enter, and he rests his head on the steering wheel. She bonks him on the head with the flat of her broadsword.

"Houston, Clyde. Remember? We're going to Houston."

"Godammit... You ruined it. You fucking ruined it." He turns the key to the ignition and they pull out of the parking lot. Hunched over. Defeated. But still so very angry. He grinds his teeth as they exit Breaux Bridge, driving off into the night. He swears to himself that he won't get discouraged. That he'll still be the one to end her. He raises that same chilling smile. An all-timer. It'll be an all-timer. He's been waiting such a long time for this. A bloodlust he hasn't felt since his first kill, all those years ago. As he sits there grinning and grinding his teeth, she kicks her feet up onto the dashboard and sighs.

"No more getting distracted, Clyde." She nods off in the truck, and in her dreams finds herself back there. The gray, hallowed place where she came from. A woman stands across from her, with long black hair and hazel eyes. The violence and screaming that surrounded her, as she stood trapped there in a haze. She wakes up sweating, Clyde looking at her with contempt.

"I guess neither of us are sleeping tonight, huh Lady No-Name?"

CHAPTER 6: SELF-SABOTAGE

Matt paces around his office, muttering under his breath as he drowns himself in top-shelf whiskey. The fog looms over Dallas, cloaking the city that Matt gazes over so often. He looks upwards through the window pane, the light that changes him gone for far too long. He staggers over to his desk, clutching his wife's photo and staring longingly for her. If only she understood.

Mason Industries, a castle his father left him that he finds crumbling beneath him. A man of self-sabotage, Matt Bowen craves fulfillment of the most basic of urges. He has spiraled over the last year, indulging himself far too much. He staggers out of his office and onto the main floor, where Leah waits nervously behind her desk.

"Leah! Has she called? Please, please tell me she has."

Leah puts her hand on her forehead and sighs. "The answer

is still no, sir. I'm sorry. I can tell you miss her." Matt groans and staggers back into his office, clenching his bottle of whiskey. He takes a swig of whiskey and collapses into his office chair, his hands over his face.

"Emma... why do you do this to me?" He weeps at his desk in his drunken state. "You just don't get... you saw who I really am. And you rejected me!" He cries, clutching his wife's photo as he wallows in self-pity. Matt Bowen, the man behind the monster. He longs for his wife as much as he longs for the fog to lift, for the moonlight to return. Matt Bowen, at this moment, is just a man.

He hates being a man, so weak and fragile. Prone to the sadness and self-loathing that human beings are. He takes another swig of whiskey and staggers over to the window pane, gazing into the fog.

"Fuck you! Fuck this! Fuck my life!" He nurses his bottle of whiskey as he curls up onto the floor, passing out in his drunken stupor. As he fades away he curses his father, his job, and his affliction that pushed Emma away.

Leah gets up from her desk and peers into Matt's office, seeing him laying sprawled on his back on the floor. She walks up to him and delicately turns him on his side. She sighs and heads for the break room, where Bill stands sipping on his cup of coffee.

"So what's new with Bowen?" Bill smirks as he leans against the counter.

"I just found him passed out on the floor in his office. I had to flip him on his side, I couldn't just leave him there like that." Leah replies, as she fills her styrofoam cup with coffee. "He's such a sad man. I can't help but feel bad for him."

Bill furrows his brow as he takes another sip. "You shouldn't feel bad for Matt Bowen, Leah. He's a victim of his own design. He's plunged this company into the red, and it's only a matter of time before he's sacked. You shouldn't cling to him, Leah. Or else he could take you down with him."

Leah scowls over at Bill. "I don't cling to him, Bill. I'm his secretary. It's my job to see to his needs. It's amazing anything's getting done around here. And you can bet your ass Bill, I'm just as ready for him to leave as you are."

Bill chuckles as he tosses his styrofoam cup in the trash. "The man's time is running out. I'm glad to hear you're just as ready as I am, Leah." He walks away, back to his office. "You know, that fog is supposed to lift in a few days. Things will change around here, sooner rather than later."

Leah finishes her coffee and walks back to her desk. Matt Bowen. What a pitiful, sorry excuse for a boss. But Leah can't help but feel sorry for him. A victim of his own design. So tragic. There is nothing more devastating, Leah thinks to herself, than a man who orchestrates his own demise.

As the hours pass by, Leah takes her leave, and Matt finds himself alone in his office, waking up on the floor with the smell of whiskey spilled on the carpet. He stands up and heaves, his head throbbing and his insides turning. He picks up the bottle of whiskey, holding it up to his eyes, and finds that one last shot remains. He takes a final swig, his breath relaxing as it runs down his throat. He heads for the elevator, and Owen the night guard stands there waiting, furrowing his brow at Matt.

"Not your best of nights, sir?" Owen remarks, as Matt turns and glares at him.

"You should watch your fucking mouth, Owen."

"I'm sorry Matt. About everything. About your wife." Owen tilts his head down. "But the path you're on, the drinking, you're headed toward rock bottom. Jails, institutions, or death, Matt. That's what's waiting for you."

"More baloney from your fucking meetings. Piss off." Matt enters the elevator and leans against the side of it, covering his face as he descends to the ground floor. He exits, seeing his limo parked, waiting for him. He turns the corner, walking away from it, and paces through the fog on the streets of the city of Dallas.

Hands in his pockets, he staggers down the street, the streetlights glaring in his eyes as he turns his head down. He walks further, groaning as the cars pass by and and the lights of local businesses start to turn off. As he reaches further he smells the musk of cigarette smoke and looks upon a bar, lights on and patrons chattering. *Morgan's Tavern.* He walks into the bar and takes a seat at the counter, as the bartender approaches him.

"Bourbon. Neat. Leave the bottle." He sighs as he looks around the bar. What a dive. Lowlifes meander around the room, playing pool and smoking cigarettes. He sighs, rueful of the place he's found himself in. The bartender returns with his bourbon and he takes a long swig, closing his eyes as his muscles relax. A man passing by puts his hand on the counter, looming over Matt as he exhales cigarette smoke onto him.

"What's some rich pretty boy like you doing in here?"

Matt turns to the thug, scowling and baring his teeth. "You don't want to fuck with me. Step off."

The man cackles as the bartender looks away, putting his hand on Matt's shoulder and leaning over. "You looking for a fight? I hate types like you. Thinking you're better than everyone in here. You're a barfly, just like us. But I can tell from the look on your face... you think this place is just some dump."

Matt swings at the man, hitting him square in the face. But he still stands there, glaring at Matt. And he smiles. He punches Matt in the eye, knocking him off his stool and onto the floor. The man stomps on Matt's ribs, kicking him over and over. As Matt loses consciousness, the thug growls and looks into Matt. "Stay the fuck out of my bar!"

Matt awakens hours later, outside on the pavement, with a black eye and a stinging pain in his side. His suit trashed, his watch and wallet gone. He looks up and howls, "I hate this fucking city!"

CHAPTER 7: THE NOISE

"Randall! You're running late! Make sure you get to work on time!" Zoe yells from across the house. Randall wakes up startled in his bed, rolling off the mattress and onto the floor.

"...Yeah, Mom! Got it." He picks himself up and throws on his orange employee vest, rushing for the kitchen as his mother places his breakfast upon the kitchen table..

"Eggs and bacon this morning, Randall. Better eat it fast," Zoe tells him. Randall wolfs down his breakfast, and places a cigarette in his mouth as he heads out the door. Zoe looks over at Randall with a look of annoyance.

"...Thanks! Thanks for the breakfast, Mom."

Zoe rolls her eyes as Randall continues out the door. "You're welcome, sweetie. For the breakfast. But hold on! We should talk more about community college. You still can go there. You don't have to keep waking up at 5 AM every morning, rushing out of the house. You can have a better life, sweetie."

Randall sighs as he exits the house and puts on his black baseball cap. "I'm happy with my life, Mom. And I'm tired of people telling me otherwise." He lights his cigarette on the way out the door, as he walks down Henderson road. He twirls his cigarette, watching the smoke dance in the early morning air. As he approaches the gas station, he ashes his cigarette and walks into the store. Gertie waits for him behind the counter.

"Randall! Right up to the minute. Glad you could make it today."

"Thanks for that, Gertie," Randall replies. "I had a hard time last night.

"Anything you want to talk about, honey?"

"No, Gertie, it's not anything that important," he replies.

"Could you be a dear and clean out the men's room? We want to make sure that it's spic and span before customers arrive," Gertie tells him.

"Sure thing, Gertie," Randall replies. Randall grabs the store's spray bottle and heads into the men's bathroom, wiping down the mirror and then the seats. He checks the flystrip hanging from the ceiling, but finds not a single fly stuck to the paper. "That's strange..." he mutters. "This thing should be covered with them."

As the store opens, customers begin to pile in, with Randall constantly at the register ringing out orders and wiping down the counter. Randall sometimes feels like he might as well be working at a factory, stuck on an assembly line doing the same thing, over and over again. The menial tasks become almost rhythmic, the chiming of the register and the same one-off responses he gives to the customers becoming a loop of monotony. As the day passes by, Randall becomes more and more uneasy.

The constant chiming of the door, the customer complaints, and the ringing of the cash register turn into a noise, a noise he can't get out of his head. A constant drone that blacks everything else out, leaving Randall at the register jittering, his hands trembling and his head throbbing. The noise only rings louder and louder, until he can feel it in his muscles, and even in his bones.

Racing thoughts, rumination. He is left at the register with no means of coping, customers constantly walking up to the counter. His thoughts slowly decline into a jumbled mess, his pace and attention wavering with every new transaction. College, a career, a house and a car. All things that remain out of sight, but something he feels nothing but shame and remorse for delaying over and over again.

The noise intensifies as he begins to sweat, wiping his brow as he continues to ring-out customers. One step short from panicking, Randall's cheery attitude that he puts on for his job becomes one of annoyance and agitation. He lurches over the counter as the noise dials up further, his hands shaking beyond belief.

"Gertie! I'm going out for my smoke break!" He rushes outside and desperately removes his cigarettes from his shirt pocket, nearly dropping the pack as he fumbles about for his lighter. He lights his cigarette, and takes one long drag. And the noise dials back. He stands there, puffing on it as it dials back further and further. With each passing hit the volume lowers, until he's just standing there, holding his lit cigarette in his hand. From agony to bliss. He looks upon the field across the street, but does not see his heron friend in the grass. Even the bird has left town.

CHAPTER 8: ASPHYXIATION

"Houston! Here we are, you stupid bitch." Clyde leans over the steering wheel, desperately trying to keep his eyes open. "Godammit! I'm fucking tired. We need to stop somewhere. I need a fucking break."

"It's the middle of the day, Clyde. You can wait until bedtime," she replies.

"We need to stop somewhere! I gotta rest my eyes," Clyde whines.

They approach a large, dusty truck stop, with a large roadside bar waiting for them.

"Let's stop here," she tells him. "You can rest your eyes, and I can have a drink."

They pull into the parking lot, and she exits the truck as

Clyde quickly falls asleep in the driver's seat. She enters the bar, broadsword holstered to her back, and sits herself down on a stool.

"I'll have a shot of Daniels," she tells the bartender. She eyes the surrounding bar patrons, as they play pool and drink merrily. The bartender slides over her shot, and she knocks it back without spilling a drop. She sits there, lingering as afternoon sunlight fades. She knocks back one last shot before paying her tab and walks out of the roadside bar, into the parking lot where Clyde remains asleep in the driver's seat.

She smacks him on the back of the head.

"Hey! What the fuck! Completely unprovoked! You bitch!"

"Let's get a move on, Clyde," she says. "We'll find a motel for the night."

"Finally!" Clyde turns the key to the ignition and they drive off from the truck stop and into the city of Houston. They drive for miles and miles, not a cloud in the sky, and the sun beats down on the road ahead of them. They stop at a dingy motel deep in the city, a place where they can rent a room with no questions asked. She enters the motel room, broadsword holstered to her back. Clyde locks his truck and enters as she sits down on the couch. He glares at her and grits his teeth.

"So we made it! Finally here in Godamm Houston. Fuck, I hate the weather here! And here we are, sitting around in another Godamm motel. You mind telling me what we're doing now?"

"Getting some rest, Clyde," she replies. "We've got a big day tomorrow. You should relax for the rest of the evening."

Clyde grimaces at her, glaring with hate in his eyes. "You know something, Lady No-Name? You remind me of someone. From a long time ago. She was so much fun. The things I did to her. The way she screamed. She was my favorite toy." He walks in front of her, blocking the view of the television. "It took so, so long to break her. But when she did, God, I was so satisfied. That taste, from her torture, it's what's kept me going for all these years. I've had a long, prolific career as a killer. And it's not ending here, in this shitty motel in Houston."

She leans forward from the couch and looks into Clyde, with her gray-blue eyes. "You should watch your mouth, Clyde," she tells him. "If not, I can shut it for you."

Clyde laughs as he paces around the room, staring into her like the predator he is. "I think right now... I'm gonna strangle you. Watch the lights go out in those Godamm ugly fucking eyes of yours."

He rushes toward her, scrambling over to the couch. She leaps up and kicks him square in the face, and he tumbles backwards, tangling himself in the motel curtain.

"Godammit! You're like a fucking ninja! Let me at you! I'll kill you here and now!"

She grabs the curtain cord and fastens it around his neck, pulling tightly in both directions.

"You don't fucking learn!" she screams. "I could kill you right here! You could die, in this shitty motel, at the hands of a woman half your size! You fucking coward." He scratches at his throat as he gasps for air, his eyes bloodshot as he looks into hers. She bares her teeth, her eyes looking into him like daggers. "You should be worried about your time, Clyde. It's drawing near to an end. But not now." She relaxes her grip as he pulls away from her, standing up and heaving, hacking his lungs out with his hands on his knees.

"That fight in you, bitch. That rage. It fuels me. Clyde hobbles over to the bedroom, and collapses on the bed. "You take the couch, right?"

She sighs as she sits back down and turns on the television. She flips to the news, her first target right there on the screen.

"Councilman Carver, you've denied any connection to the

misconduct of Mason Industries in the construction of the Hibiscus Park Affordable Housing Development. State investigators say otherwise. What do you have to say to the people of Houston?"

"My only objective in the construction of Hibiscus Park has been to ensure that economically disadvantaged citizens of this city have access to quality housing. I myself am abhorred by the conduct of Mason Industries. My team is cooperating with the state investigation, and I can assure the people of this city that I will be acquitted. No further comment."

She leans back on the couch and kicks her feet up on the coffee table. "You're time's coming, Councilman Carver. Fucking monster." As the night passes on, she dozes off on the couch, finding herself in a deep slumber.

In her dreams, she finds herself back there. In that place, a place gray and violent. A place where she could scream, and nobody could hear her. A place so terrifying, she couldn't breathe. And the woman in the black cloak who stood across from her there, with long black hair and hazel eyes. A place where she could not lay a hand on the horrors that surrounded her. She opens her eyes and screams. The waking nightmare drones on.

CHAPTER 9: CRAVING

Jacqueline wakes up in her bed, having been called in late to the private office, to work overtime for Councilman Carver. She enjoys working for such a charismatic man. His thick, gray hair, his fierce blue eyes, and an attitude that she finds so enthralling. Her bedroom, in her studio apartment, is decorated with tokens of the Carver campaign. Election signs and memorabilia decorate the walls. She hops in the shower, humming to herself, excited for another day on the job.

She gathers her things and walks out the door, cheerfully entering her car and driving off on her way to the office. As she drives down the road, she smiles. She pulls into the parking lot, and exits her car with a joyful pep in her step. Jacqueline walks into the private office, purse over her shoulder and a nervous smile on her face. The office receptionist, Alice, lingers by the water cooler.

"There you are, Jacqueline. Another fucking day working for Councilman Carver, huh?"

"I don't know why you're always so gloomy, Alice," Jacqueline replies. "I like working here. John Carver is a good man."

"Oh please, I don't know why you always say that about him. He's a deranged, corrupt cokehead."

Jacqueline fills her cup with water from the cooler. "John works so hard for all of us. And the city! That's just what you have to put up with, working for politicians."

Alice smirks over at her. "You know, that phobia of the sun he has. Pretty freaky. And you're far from his first assistant."

"John's debilitated by his phobia, and he still comes to work every day," Jacqueline replies. "That's why I admire the man so much."

"Listen, these are just rumors, but his last two assistants? They both 'suddenly resigned' Never saw them again."

"And why should I care, Alice?" Jacqueline asks sarcastically.

"Why should you care?" Alice sets down her cup of water. "Jacqueline, I've always thought there's something wrong with you. Those other assistants hated working for him. You seem to idolize the man. You need to be careful. I wouldn't trust Carver farther than I could throw him."

"That's why I'm his assistant, and you're just the receptionist," Jacqueline replies.

"You truly are irredeemable, aren't you Jacqueline?"

"And you're an old bitch," Jacqueline snaps back.

"That does it then!" Alice exclaims as she turns away. "Maybe you should watch your neck, you young thing."

Jacqueline smiles as Alice walks away. It's not that John Carver is a good man. But his ferocity, his ruthlessness, these things excite her. The cocaine, the anger, the look in his eyes. John Carver is a bad man. And Jacqueline likes bad men. Always has. For a woman who feels so empty inside, the excitement of being with someone who breaks every rule, doesn't take shit from anyone, she just finds it so thrilling. To be with a villain.

Jacqueline goes into the back office, and prepares John's cocaine. Piling it onto his glass tray, she smiles as she prepares him his criminal vice. She picks up the tray and heads over to John's office, walking with a cheery stride in her step. She opens John's office door as he sits there, waiting for her.

"Right on time, Jacqueline," John tells her. "I don't know what I'd do without you."

Jacqueline smiles as she places his cocaine on his desk. "Oh sir, I wouldn't forget like I did last time. The work you do, it's so important."

John smiles at her as he begins cutting lines of his cocaine. "Excellent, Jacqueline. I know I can always count on you."

"Of course, sir! Absolutely."

Jacqueline exits John's office and returns back to her desk. She toils away for the rest of the day, shaking with excitement. The possibilities, the evil in him, prove distracting. She chews on the end of her pen, nervously trying to finish her work. As her shift draws near to an end, she sees Alice on her way out the door.

"Still got the hots for Carver?" Alice asks.

"You should watch yourself, Alice. You old thing." Jacqueline smirks on her way out the door, her purse over her shoulder as she leaves the building.

She chuckles to herself while driving home. His phobia of the sun is indeed quite peculiar. He can't even let it touch him. Jacqueline ponders to herself, what if he were a vampire? Outlandish, impossible. But a dark dream that would remake her life. John Carver, not just the man she finds herself so infatuated with, but a monster. Vampires, the essence of evil. How she longs for him. As she drives through the town, she smiles as she sees the sun going down. Imagine, a whole new world, just waiting to fulfill her fantasy.

She returns home and lays her purse down on the kitchen table. She grabs a bottle of wine from her cupboard and pours herself a glass, kicking her feet up on the coffee table before she takes a sip. She chuckles. Power within her grasp, perhaps? A chance to be with such a man. Possibly for eternity. Jacqueline has always wanted to do bad things. To be with a bad man, to commit such vile acts.

She has fantasized about the violence. Inflicting pain, to fill the void inside her. A woman who has been drawn to darkness, from such a young age. Her parents didn't know how to handle her, constant visits to therapists, warning about her proclivity to evil, and her being drawn to it. A ticking time bomb. She lives among people who just don't seem to get it. How infatuated with wickedness she is.

She drinks the whole bottle over the next few hours and retires to bed. She lays there, tossing and turning, giggling to herself as she falls asleep. Her shot for obtaining something truly unholy. A woman drawn to sin, she craves the creature in him.

CHAPTER 10: ONCE BITTEN

Jacqueline twirls her hair at her desk as she waits anxiously for John to arrive. Today's the day that she'll ask him that question. A new life, a new chance at greatness. How she craves what John has. She chuckles as she eyes Alice, from down the hall.

"Good morning, Alice. I trust you made it here safely?"

"I made it here just fine, Jacqueline," Alice replies.

"You still terrified of Councilman Carver?" Jacqueline asks, with a smirk on her face.

"I'm telling you Jacqueline, you should keep away from him as much as you can."

"Noted, and ignored," Jacqueline replies.

"I've tried my best with you, Jacqueline. You've been warned." Alice sits down at her desk with a sigh. "Some people just won't listen."

Jacqueline smiles as she sees John enter the door, closing his umbrella and heading straight for his office. She stands up and goes into the back room, to prepare his cocaine. She piles it onto the glass tray and walks over to John's office, knocking on the door.

"Come in," John answers. Jacqueline opens the door and places John's cocaine on his desk.

"Always happy to see you, sir," Jacqueline tells him.

"I could say the same for you," John replies.

"You work so hard, you know. I can't believe it. You really do care for your work, don't you sir?"

John smiles as he cuts up his cocaine. "All for the city of Houston, my dear. I'll admit, it takes its toll on me."

"It must be awfully lonely, sir. You're here all day, cooped up in your office by yourself. If you ever needed company, you know I'm right here."

John looks up at Jacqueline, an eerie grin on his face. "You know, Jacqueline, if you're not doing anything tonight, I'd be delighted to have you over for a nightcap."

Jacqueline bends over and puts her hand on his desk. "You know sir, if I didn't know any better, I'd think you were a vampire!"

John grins ear to ear as he gazes into Jacqueline's eyes. "And what if I am, Jacqueline?"

Jacqueline giggles with excitement. She pours it on thick. "Oh sir, I would want nothing more than for you to turn me! I've been so loyal, and you're so handsome! I could be so much more than your assistant..." She leans over and caresses his neck. "I could be your woman. If time would let me."

John laughs as he snorts a line of cocaine. "Jacqueline, honey, I think I may just take the rest of the day off! Here, have yourself a line." He hands Jacqueline his metal straw, and she snorts a line of cocaine. "Come along with me, why don't you? Back to my estate." John takes Jacqueline by the arm and strides out of the office, unfurling his umbrella as they walk toward the black SUV. Eddie greets them as they enter the vehicle.

"Heading home early, sir? And I see you have company."

"Oh, Eddie, me and Jacqueline here are heading back to... have a special appointment." John and Jacqueline both snicker as Eddie drives away, and they both lean in for a kiss as Eddie puts the privacy window up. "Jacqueline, just you wait. It'll be a whole new world, a whole new life! You won't regret this."

"Oh, John! I'm so glad you chose me! I've always wanted to! Will I get to... to drink blood? The blood of other people?"

"Yes, Jacqueline!" John responds. "And it's your choice. Turn them, or drain them empty!" They both laugh uproariously as Eddie pulls through the security gate, the guard tipping his hat at them. "Just you wait, Jacqueline. We're almost there."

They pull onto the estate and they both exit the SUV, arms around each other as they enter inside. The curtains are drawn, and the whole residence is lit by an array of lamps. John and Jacqueline giggle to each other as they sit down on his couch.

John laughs as he extends his fangs. "Tell me, Jacqueline. What's the first thing you're going to do, once you're a vampire?"

Jacqueline gasps in awe. Her darkest dream came true. A chance for an eternity of violence. "Oh! I'll go after Alice! That bitch! I'll bleed her dry. I'm ready, sir!" Jacqueline exclaims. "Do it! Turn me!"

"Very well then," John replies. Jacqueline tilts her head to the side as John sinks his fangs into her, Jacqueline smiling as he drinks her blood. Her blood flows through John's fangs, and his eyes become dilated, feeling the euphoria from drinking her blood.

"I'm so excited! I'm so excited, sir!"

John continues drinking her blood, gorging himself as the minutes pass by. Jacqueline's face slowly becomes pale. Her smile droops, and her arms and legs become heavy. She lets out a whimper as John continues draining her.

"...Sir? What... are you doing?"

John drains her and drains her, until her smile droops and the light goes out in her eyes. And he sits there drinking, still drawing her blood, until her life is snuffed out. John grabs her body by the hair, and drags her across the living room floor. He walks down the steps to his basement, her body banging on the steps as he drags her down .

An open furnace waits there for John, and he flings her in by her hair. Her body becomes scorched by the flames, her skin blackening as she burns away. John walks up to the furnace and closes the door. He dusts off his hands and walks away, his dark desire fulfilled.

CHAPTER 11: YOU'RE NOT SUPPOSED TO BE HERE

Clyde sits nervously in the motel room, awkwardly silent as he knows she's just a few feet away. Drying her hands, she walks out of the bathroom, broadsword holstered to her back.

"Time to go for a drive, Clyde. Get yourself ready."

"Another day!" Clyde yells. "Another day stuck with Lady No-Name, driving around aimlessly and getting wacked with that fucking sword. Your time's coming, bitch."

"Cram it, Clyde. There's work to be done today." She walks out the door, Clyde trailing behind as they enter his pickup truck. They head onto the road, and she signals the directions to Clyde until they approach a large, gated neighborhood.

"This place is upscale, Lady No-Name. We're not getting in

here. Not in your wildest dreams."

She chuckles and she exits the truck, as the neighborhood guard exits his booth to check on the commotion. She removes her broadsword with just her right hand, and slams it onto the head of the guard. He instantaneously drops to the ground, unconscious. She walks into the guard booth and opens the gate, then walks back to the truck triumphantly, entering as Clyde shudders. Clyde stares at her, shocked at the turn of events.

"You bitch! You came here to kill, didn't you? We're not getting away with it here! He quickly puts the truck in reverse, but then finds her broadsword at his neck.

"Keep driving, Clyde. If you want to live another day." He puts the truck back into drive and they roll into the neighborhood, Clyde cursing under his breath as they approach John Carver's estate.

"Okay, what now, bitch? We're here! What do you expect me to do?" he cries.

She slams Clyde's head into the steering wheel, over and over again, until he falls limp. She pulls the key from the ignition and exits, locking both doors to the truck. She walks up the hill onto John's estate, holding her broadsword in her right hand, to find Eddie, leaning against the SUV and smoking a cigar.

"You come here to play with Councilman Carver?" He laughs, ashing his cigar onto the driveway and walking up to her. "He's busy with another girl right now, but I can let him know you're waiting." He gestures his cigar at her broadsword. "You here to do a little roleplay?"

"You're not supposed to be here yet!" She exclaims.

She grabs his cigar, and presses its lit end into his forehead.

"Ouch! You bitch! You fucking bitch!"

She slashes her broadsword into his chest. Eddie falls backward onto the driveway, bleeding and writhing.

"You whore! You crazy whore! Where the fuck did you get that thing?"

She kneels over him. She holds her sword in two hands, and presses it into his heart. The light goes out in his eyes. She removes it, carrying it into Carver's home, the curtains inside drawn. She paces into the living room and hears a loud snort, coming from his study.

"Who the fuck is here now?" John exits his study, wiping cocaine off his lip and staring at her, holding her bloody broadsword in her right hand, looking into him. "Oh, fuck. Not one of you people."

She rushes at him, and he dodges to the left as she swings her sword at him. He extends his fingernails and slashes at her face, blood splattering from her cheek onto the wall. She elbows him in the stomach, knocking him back, and turns to kick him square in the chest. He falls against the wall, eyes fierce and fangs extended. He leaps at her, and she slashes her sword upward, lopping his right arm off. He staggers backward, and she approaches, cutting into him and lopping off his other arm. He falls backward onto his living room carpet, bleeding out and cursing at her.

"Fuck you! Bitch! You got me! There's a million and one ways to kill a vampire! So what's it gonna be, huh?" he taunts her, defiantly.

She opens the third zipper on her black leather jacket, and removes the pair of pliers, purchased at the hardware store in Mississippi. She kneels over him and yanks out one fang, and then the other. He lays there enraged. "Oh! Hilarious! Fucking hilarious! They'll grow back, you bitch! Is that all you got?"

She holds her broadsword in two hands. With complete precision, she removes his jaw. He lays there, gurgling on his own blood, drowning in the very thing he's killed for. As he stares into the ceiling, he regrets nothing.

She walks down the stairs of his basement, to find Jacqueline burning in the furnace. She looks at her, and lets out a deep, grievous sigh. She holsters her broadsword and turns off the furnace. As she exits, she leaves the third zipper open.

She walks down the driveway and back into the truck, slapping Clyde across the head. He wakes up groaning, dribbling spit and crying.

"Time to go, bud. Back to the motel. I'm finished here."

CHAPTER 12: DO NOT CALL ME BUDDY

Clyde sits in the motel room, anxiously watching the news. She sleeps only a few feet away in the bedroom, and he shakes with nervousness as the local news plays.

"This just in! Houston City Councilman John Carver has been found dead in his home! His driver was also found dead in the driveway, and a third, unidentified victim found burned postmortem in his furnace! Stranger still, Authorities say that forensics teams have found defensive wounds on the victims, consistent with that of a broadsword! We have with us here Houston Chief of Police, Trent Dreyer."

"What has happened here today is an atrocity, and a sad day for the city of Houston, and Texas. We have a confirmed eyewitness report saying the assailant was a woman, aged 20-26, with brown hair and gray-blue eyes. There was also an accomplice, a bald, stout man driving a black pickup truck. Councilman Carver's estate does

contain surveillance cameras, but our investigators are at a loss due to a lack of footage. It's as if they've never been turned on. We ask any citizens of Houston who have information to call in any tips they have. We may be looking at a serial killer here, folks. A broadsword killer."

Clyde jumps up and races into the bedroom, where she lays on the bed, legs crossed. "You crazy bitch! You're insane! That guy was high-profile! We're dead! We're fucking dead! What's keeping me here? Huh? Stuck with you?"

She looks at him, and smirks. "I am Clyde. I'm keeping you here."

Clyde growls and turns away from her. "I'm grabbing the keys to the truck. I'm out of here!"

She laughs and sneers at Clyde. "I won't stop you. Not this time, buddy."

Clyde runs out of the motel room and hops into the truck, racing down the road and cursing under his breath. He drives and he drives, sweating profusely and shaking with fear. "He pulls off onto the side of the road, exiting the truck and pacing back and forth, muttering under his breath. "That bitch! She made a fool out of me! A fucking fool!" He grinds his teeth, shaking and sweating, before becoming freakishly still. "I just need to kill again! That's it! I'll kill again. That'll do it for me! I need that feeling again!"

He goes back into the truck and continues down the road, driving for miles and miles. He finds himself at the same truck stop from when they arrived in Houston. He exits the truck and spies a black-haired woman, walking around the side of the bar. His breathing becomes rapid. His hands shake with excitement. And he follows her, as she turns the corner around the bar. But then he stops. His breathing slows again. His hands stop shaking.

"Godammit! Godammit! She's not her! She's not fucking her! I can't do it! I can't fucking do it!"

A large, bearded trucker, scratching the back of his head, approaches Clyde. "Everything okay, buddy?"

Clyde turns to the man with a furious look on his face. "Don't fucking call me that! Do *not* call me buddy!"

The trucker furrows his brow. "You looking for trouble?"

Clyde relaxes his breathing and lets out a deep sigh. "I apologize for my outburst. And as a matter of fact, I am. Do you know where I can get a gun? Unregistered. And quick."

The trucker smiles and pulls out his cellphone. "I know a guy. You can meet him in the truck lot."

Clyde heads over to the truck lot, pacing back and forth and muttering under his breath. A man in a baseball cap and sunglasses approaches him. "You needed something?"

"Yeah. A gun. Revolver, if you have one," Clyde tells him.

"Wait here." The dealer replies, turning the corner as Clyde waits anxiously. He returns bearing a revolver and a box of ammunition. "$300. Cash?"

"Let me see it first," Clyde replies, snatching it out of the dealer's hands.

"Hold up, fuckhead!" The dealer reaches for a gun holstered at his side, but not before Clyde pistol-whips him across the head, and he drops to the ground. Clyde picks up the box of ammunition and runs for his pickup truck, shaking as he puts the keys in the ignition and races out of the truck stop.

He drives along cackling, racing down the road back to the motel. "I've got her! I've finally got that bitch!" As he pulls into the motel parking lot, he loads a round into each of the six chambers. "I hate using these things. So Godamm impersonal."

He storms the motel room, firing all six shots into the bed. But no blood spills. He pulls off the blanket to find pillows stacked on top of each other. He looks to the side and sees her there, proudly holding her broadsword in her right hand. She runs at him and bonks him on the head with the flat of her broadsword.

"You bitch! You fucking bitch!" He runs back out of the motel room and onto the sidewalk, but stops dead, snarling and trembling. He turns around to see her standing across from him, her blue-gray eyes piercing into his.

"You bitch! Standing there like you're some Godamm hero! You're not, you know. We're the same! You're cruel, you're inventive, and you're merciless! You're an expert killer in your own right! We're the same! We're the fucking same! We're both evil motherfuckers!"

"I'm not evil. And neither are you, Clyde."

"What the fuck did you just say to me?" he sneers.

"You are sick. You are diseased. And you are helpless."

"That's a load! That's a fucking load of bullshit!" he screams.

"I'll say it again," she replies. "You are sick, diseased, and helpless. But you're not evil, bud."

He wails and rushes toward her, arms flailing at her. She holds her sword in two hands. And she runs him through. She pushes him off her sword, and he collapses onto the ground, teeth stained with his own blood.

"Do it. Call me evil. You cunt!"

"No, Clyde, you're not evil. And nobody else will ever say you were." She takes the truck keys off of Clyde, and enters the driver's side. She turns the key to the ignition, and drives away.

As Clyde lays there, he sobs. He sobs and he sobs, dribbling blood onto his shirt as the light fades out. To die ignored. To die unremembered. To die ordinary.

As she drives her hands clench the steering wheel, and she heads for the highway, to Dallas. As the sunlight fades, the truck sputters and slows. She pulls off onto the side and looks at the fuel gauge, empty.

"God fucking dammit!" She exits the truck and runs down the highway. She runs for hours, until she comes across a roadside gas station. She fills a can of gas with haste and runs back to the truck. As the hours have passed, it is already night. She fills up the truck and enters, putting the pedal to the floor.

CHAPTER 13:
CHASING A BUZZ

Matt paces around his office, shaking and clutching his bottle of whiskey. He chugs from the bottle, his blonde hair haggard and his tie loosened. He nurses his black eye as he gazes through the windowpane. A broken man chasing a buzz he lost long ago. He wipes the sweat off his brow and walks over to his desk, clutching his wife's photo. He takes a final swig before setting the bottle down at the desk, approaching the window with a look of nervousness reflected in his face.

It is past midnight, and the fog still looms. Matt turns away, prepared to take his leave. He walks down the hall, toward the elevator, to see Owen waiting for it to open.

"Sir! I'm just on my way down to do my night rounds." He pauses and looks upon Matt's face. He sighs and looks back at the elevator. "I've already told you my advice, Matt. I'll skip the speech tonight."

"I don't know if I could handle another one, Owen." Matt wipes the sweat off his brow as the elevator door opens. They both enter, standing awkwardly as they reach the bottom floor. As they exit the building and into the parking lot, the fog starts to lift.

"Would you look at that, sir?" Owen chuckles. "It looks like we're out of the storm."

Little by little, the fog lifts, and the light pierces through from a bright, waxing moon, almost full. Matt writhes in agony. His bones snap and break, his muscles tear and then heal. A snout protrudes, and coarse, brown fur erupts from his skin. He stands there, a giant beast howling into the darkness. It traps Owen in its gaze.

"Holy shit! You're a Godamm werewolf!" Owen stumbles back, draws his gun and fires square into the beast's chest. The bullet ricochets off, failing to pierce the thick hide. The beast slashes at Owen's throat, and Owen collapses, bleeding out onto the pavement. Writhing on the ground, Owen still reaches for his radio. The beast stomps on Owen's hand and then his head, sending shrapnel from his skull flying and splattering his brains onto the pavement. A scream echoes from across the parking lot. Leah stands quivering, desperately trying to jam her keys into her car. The beast approaches Leah, knocking her onto the ground with a single swing of its arm.

"What are you? What have you done with Matt? You monster!"

The beast looms over her and snarls. "I am him. How do you like me now?" The beast hoists her over one shoulder, and returns to hoist Owen's corpse over the other. Leah slaps and kicks at him, screaming at the top of her lungs.

"Matt... please. You don't have to do this. I know you're in there! I know it! Matt! Matthew Bowen! Stop this! Now!"

The beast bares its teeth. "I've been waiting so long to do this to you, Leah." It tosses her back onto the pavement and smacks her across the face, and she falls unconscious. Leah awakens on the side of an old dirt road, being dragged into the woods by the beast. "Please Matt! Please!" she screams, as it drags her further and further into the brush.

It tears into her, ripping and snarling, pulling out her organs and eating them, as she looks upon it in horror. Before she falls limp, she looks next to her, to see Owen's corpse sprawled across from her. She falls dead in the dirt. The beast leaves her there, and storms off into the night. It has its fill until morning.

Matt staggers into his office as the sun comes up, shaking and sweating. He grabs a bottle of whiskey, and chugs insatiably until not a single drop remains. He grabs his wife's photo and collapses onto the floor, curling up and crying.

"It doesn't feel as good... It doesn't feel as good!" His cries turn to laughter, as he rocks back and forth on the floor. "Tomorrow! Tomorrow it will be full!" He peers into his wife's photo. "Tomorrow... you'll get what's coming to you! Bitch! Tramp! Whore!" He cackles maniacally, as he smashes the photo.

CHAPTER 14:
THERE HE LIES

Matt stands in his office gazing into the full moon, a werewolf that has reached his full form. Towering in his office, he howls and he howls. Tonight's the night that Emma will get what's coming to her. He'll break her bones first. Then rip into her, eating organ after organ, saving her heart for last. And then he'll tear her apart, just for fun. Howling into the night, he gazes into the moon, intoxicated by it. He stands there ready again, ready to kill, not just to scratch the itch, but to fulfill a vile vendetta.

His office door is kicked in, startling him. Holding her broadsword in her right hand, she brushes her brown hair aside as she stares him down in her black leather jacket. He turns at her and laughs.

"Oh! One of you people. How funny. Tonight, of all nights. I'll tear you apart, bitch." He lunges at her and swings his claws toward her. She slashes at him with her broadsword, but with no effect. He slams her into his desk, knocking it over and sending her tumbling over it.

"You bitch." He snarls. "Are you sure you're cut out for this?"

"You're a monster, Matthew Bowen," she tells him. "And you need to be put down."

"You Godamm idiot." He laughs. "You can't put me down without a silver bullet." He smashes his desk, sending pieces of wood flying, and she turns and crouches to shield herself from the debris. She sees his bottle of whiskey, miraculously on the floor, unaffected by the violence.

She opens the fourth zipper of her jacket, and removes the book of matches. She grabs the bottle of whiskey and hurls it at his chest, the bottle smashing and the liquor splashing all over him. She lights a match, and tosses it at him. He is set aflame, and staggers around the room, disoriented and crying out.

"You bitch!" he cries. "That was a dirty trick! But still! You need a silver bullet!"

She runs at him from across the room, and plants her left foot down on the floor. With all her force, she kicks him into the glass window panes. He shatters through them, plummeting downward and downward until he smashes into the pavement. He lays there broken, staring up into the night sky, immobilized. As the minutes pass by he curses into the night.

"That bitch! The audacity! The fucking audacity!" he howls. After some minutes pass, he sees her, standing over him, her gray-blue eyes piercing his. "You still can't kill me without a silver bullet! You bitch!"

"Yes I can," she replies. "It'll just take longer." She holds her sword in two hands, and swings into his neck. She swings and she swings, until the moonlight fades and the sun comes up. There he lies, just a man.

CHAPTER 15: IT SLITHERS IN

Randall stands behind the counter in the gas station, leaning against the wall as Gertie faces the products. It has been a slow day, and Randall taps his fingers against the counter in boredom as he looks through the window, across the field, the heron still absent. Gertie looks up from the products on the aisles.

"Randall! Honey, it's been a slow day today. Why don't you head home early?"

Randall nods his head. "I appreciate it, Gertie. I'll be back tomorrow." He exits the store and walks down the road, and as he looks up, he sees a flock of birds flying out from the bayou. He looks into the waters, and does not see a gator in sight.

Randall sits on a park bench, his head in his hands, weary from the week's work. What a grind, his job, and what a tedious life. He reaches into his shirt pocket and removes his pack of cigarettes, to find only one left, broken at the edge of the filter. He sighs as tosses them in a rubbish bin. He stands up to walk away, but then feels a soft head in his lap. A stray dog with brown fur, looking into Randall hopefully.

"Oh! Hello, boy. Are you hungry?" The dog barks in confirmation. "I'll get you something to eat, boy." He walks across the street from the park to a hot dog stand, and buys a hot dog, fixings and all, for the stray mutt. He walks back and places it on the ground, the dog happily eating away as Randall scratches it behind the ears. "There you go! Is that better, boy?" The dog finishes its meal and turns to Randall, a nervous look in its eyes. It runs away, down the street away from him. Randall sighs, and he heads for home, the TV playing in the living room.

"Another confirmed death in the Broadsword Killer case, this time CEO Matthew Bowen of Mason Industries! Shortly after she is presumed to have killed her accomplice, a factory worker from Mississippi, Bowen is the fifth victim of the killer. The executive was found beheaded in the parking lot, but authorities have found themselves baffled, as eyewitness reports place the Broadsword Killer herself as having tampered with surveillance footage. We have here with us Dallas Chief of Police Jerry Anderson with more on the ongoing story."

"We want to tell the public that we don't let serial killers escape, here in Dallas. We will be cooperating with Houston PD in finding the deranged woman who committed this horrible crime. We don't know enough at this time to establish whether the killings were motivated by the Hibiscus Park construction scandal. But I can say personally that this isn't how mentally sound people resolve their grudges. Not in this fashion. We ask members of the public to call in any tips on finding The Broadsword Killer."

"Oh, it's just horrible," Zoe says, looking toward Randall. "I'm sure Matt Bowen had a lot of enemies though, with that scandal in Houston."

Randall furrows his brow, looking back at his mother. "Well, good thing we don't live in Texas, Mom." His mother chuckles as she looks back at him.

"That's one way of thinking about it, sweetie." She sighs and sits down in the kitchen, putting her hand on her forehead. "It's scary though. Knowing somebody like that is on the loose."

"I wouldn't worry too much, Mom. It's rare a monster like that walks free for too long." He turns away and heads for the door. "I'm headed to the gas station, Mom. I need another pack of cigarettes." He walks down Henderson road, waving at the people that pass by.

As he walks he finds the noise returning, the noise only he can hear, growing lounder. It buzzes in the background, making him nauseous and sweaty. His head throbbing, he picks up his pace, needing his nicotine to dial it back. He walks into the gas station, finding Gertie at the counter.

"Sorry I'm back, Gertie. Need another pack of smokes. Castle Reds, shorts, if we've got them."

"Of course, honey." Gertie removes the pack of cigarettes from the shelf and places them on the counter. Randall picks them up and starts packing them in his hand as Gertie lingers there.

"Don't you think it's strange, Gertie? The wildlife. It's like it's just disappeared."

"I've noticed that, Randall," she replies. "I like to fish, myself. Haven't been very lucky lately."

As they converse, a vile thing slithers its way out of the drain. A hideous, slimy, blood-red worm, the size of a rat, inches its way out of the drain and toward the counter, leaving a red muck in its trail. It leaps at Randall, burrowing into his skin as he screams.

"Something's in me! Something's in me, Gertie!" He writhes in pain, scratching and tearing at his skin as Gertie looks on in horror. He keeps scratching and wailing, tearing at his own skin, until he becomes freakishly still. His eyes go white. He is no longer himself.

The monster grabs Gertie by the neck, strangling her. She gasps for air, but it clenches her tighter and tighter. It snaps her neck, leaving her head at a ninety degree angle. He smashes her into the countertop, and it crumbles beneath her corpse. It extends its hand and jabs it into her, tearing into her flesh and feasting upon it, until the clothes that were once Randall's are drenched in blood. It has its fill, and then walks into the back of the store. It deletes the security footage, before taking its leave.

CHAPTER 16: THE SECOND ZIPPER

She stands in her motel room, looking upon her black leather jacket, spread out across the coffee table. She could only bring herself to leave the second zipper closed. Such vile, despicable men. She put them down, and she took their credit. Time for her to leave. As she gathers her things and prepares to exit, the local news blares on the television.

"One convenience store clerk of Henderson, Louisiana has been found dead at a local gas station! Authorities remain mute on the cause of death, but have confirmed the store's security footage was tampered with. We have here with us Henderson Chief of Police, Jack Landry. Tell us, do you think The Broadsword Killer is behind this?"

"We're not ready to reveal additional details of this case to the public at this time. Our forensics team is still currently working overtime to determine the cause of death. But rest assured that Henderson PD is on the case. We don't take kindly to murderers in this

town."

She slams her hand down on the coffee table. "Godammit! Not him! Not fucking him!" She throws on her black leather jacket and races out the door, climbing into the pickup truck and desperately turning the key to the ignition. She puts the pedal to the floor, racing through the night for hours and hours. She can't be. She can't be too late. Not another one.

After hours of driving, she speeds into Henderson and careens into the driveway of Randall's home. She exits the pickup truck, holding her broadsword in her right hand, trembling. She walks up the driveway to find the front door open. She enters, and then she sees it. The monster that still looks like him, gorging itself on Randall's mother. It turns and looks at her creepily with its big, glossy white eyes.

She rushes it, swinging her sword directly into its shoulder. The sword stops dead, making a loud thump, and does not pierce the monster's flesh. She swings again, but still, she does not make a dent in the monster. Again and again she swings, with all her might, but to no effect.

"Your kind... your kind are prey." The monster cackles. "Your kind are weak. You are worthless. I will end you. And then many others. You are a pathetic sample. I enjoy this. I look forward to so much more of it."

"What you did to him... is unforgivable. Unforgivable!" she screams. "You vermin! You fucking vermin! You're like a Godamm cockroach."

"You irritate me. I can't stand you like this. My kind, when we lay eyes on a human... It's a fixation. I cannot look at a human without finding myself starving, and filled with murderous intent. My brain is telling me to kill you, over and over. The chatter ends now."

The monster cackles and grabs her by the neck, choking and strangling her. It throws her across the room, smashing her into the wall. She crumples from the blow, and it looks at her cheekily. It wants to play with its food.

It walks up to her and grabs her hair, hoisting her up, and punches her again and again in the face. Her nose breaks and her cheekbone shatters, and she remains there, barely conscious, as it walks to the other side of the room.

Barely able to keep her eyes open, she holds her sword in two hands. The monster leaps in the air. Suddenly, the sword flashes a bright red light. It fills the room in its magnificent glow, the air spinning and tables shaking. It falls onto her sword. And the sword goes through the monster.

Finding herself with a second wind, she cradles its head, and gently removes her sword. She places Randall's body next to his mother's. She stands over them, and weeps, trembling with her sword in her hand. She grasps the second zipper on her jacket, and she opens it. She wipes away her tears and turns her back, heading out of the house.

When she walks out the door, her sword slashes through the door frame like butter. She removes her holster from her back and holds it in her hand, the same red light flashing as she clutches it. She sheathes her broadsword into the holster, and enters the truck.

There's one last thing for her to do. She turns the key to the ignition and drives away, heading for Mississippi. She drives for hours, until morning, and she finds herself back at the place where this all started. Clyde's house. She opens his shed, to find a can of gas and a filthy rag.

She takes the can of gas and walks into Clyde's house. She pours it everywhere, over the horrible room down below, over the living room, and over the room filled with women's clothing. She leads a trail of gas out of the house, and as she stands in the driveway, she lights a match, and tosses it. She gazes into the flames, her work completed.

CHAPTER 17: LIMBO

She was Clyde's first kill. His first kill, twenty years ago. She was minding her own business, walking along town when he drove up on her. With simply smooth talk and a gesture of his hands, she found herself in his truck. It was almost unfair, the way he lured her in. Some people can talk others into doing anything. He jabbed her in the neck with ketamine, injecting it and paralyzing her. He dragged her down those stairs and did unspeakable things to her. Humiliated her. Tortured her while she begged him to stop. And he kept going when she just begged for him to do it, to end her life. He brutalized her far longer than she was willing to live through it.

She found herself dead. Trapped in another plane. And that's when she met her. A reaper in a pitch-black cloak, with long black hair and hazel eyes, by the name of Wynona.

"Your time here has come to an end," Wynona told her. "Come with me. I can take you to a better place."

She looked into Wynona's hazel eyes and scowled. "I won't

leave. He did that to me. He did all those things to me. It was so horrible! So horrible! I can't let him get away with it. I'll stay here, and I'll kill him where he stands."

Wynona shook her head and looked into her gray-blue eyes. "You cannot touch anything on this material plane. Again, I beg of you to come with me. I cannot force you to. But if you stay, you will be driven into madness."

She shook her head at Wynona. "He's already driven me mad. I'm not scared. Leave me be."

"Very well then," said Wynona. "It is your choice as a mortal." Wynona disappeared, and she was left there, standing in limbo, stuck in the horrible room. She stood there for years, screaming and cursing at Clyde as he dragged down more. More women, dozens, over the course of those twenty years. She howled and she wailed, and found herself further and further disturbed by her curse.

Wynona watched over her for all those years. And slowly, despite being a reaper bound by rules of cosmic proportions, she felt sorry for her. She could not believe the rage, the commitment, to her vengeance. And one day, Wynona finally cracked. Wynona returned to the room, where she still stood screaming, and offered her a deal.

"Tell me, young woman. You have been trapped in limbo for twenty years. Do you even remember your own name?" Wynona asked her.

"No. I do not. But I will still kill that man. For what he did to me, and all those other women."

"And how would you do it?" Wynona asked.

She turned and looked Wynona dead in the eyes. "I would destroy it. I would destroy his ego! I would make sure he understood how it felt. To be humiliated. To be tortured. To lose all your dignity. I will steal from him his pride as a killer, piece by piece."

Wynona looked at her and nodded in approval. "Very well then. I will bring you back to life, under a few conditions. There are other tasks I need you to take care of. There is a vampire named John Carver in Houston. He has killed thousands over the course of hundreds of years. I need him dead. There is a werewolf by the name of Matthew Bowen in Dallas. He has killed hundreds. I need him dead. The last task is that I need a vermin, called a zuntin, exterminated. They have plagued the earth for thousands of years. The larva nests beneath a drain, at a gas station, in a town called Henderson."

"And how would I accomplish this?" she asked Wynona.

"All it will take to kill the worm is a pinch of borax. But be warned, if it takes a host, the consequences will be dire. I will imprint a dossier into your mind for the quest ahead of you. I will grant you superhuman reflexes and combat ability. The last thing I will grant you is a power called enchantment. It will allow you to make any object indestructible, and any blade sharp enough to cut through anything. You should not have to use it. And if you choose to, there are many who will seek its power. Do you accept these terms?"

"Yes, I do. Do it." She told her. So Wynona took her by the hand, and in that moment, she arose, out of the blood spilled by dozens.

CHAPTER 18: I HATE THAT NAME

She lays sprawled in bed in yet another motel room, nursing her injuries. She does not know what to do next, and she groans in pain and anguish. She has suffered enough. And so have so many others. If only she could snuff out all the evil on this earth. As she lays there, the local news plays in the background. And then she hears it.

"New developments in the Broadsword Killer case! The serial killer remains at large, but has now been identified as Susan Sharp, a woman who went missing over twenty years ago! Authorities are baffled at what her motive could possibly be, and even more strange, she looks remarkably the same as she did when she went missing! The suspect was last seen in Henderson, Louisiana, and federal investigators now attribute her responsible for three homicides in the town! This brings her grand kill total to eight dead!"

She screams into her pillow in the motel room. Susan Sharp.

That's what her name was. But she cries out for a different reason. "Broadsword Killer... I hate that name."

"In other news, CEO of Senior Villas, Frank Bartrude, has been released from prison, after having served three months for a medical malpractice scandal that shook the nation. The chain of nursing homes, located in Kansas City, was found to be institutionally corrupt. Elderly residents of the nursing homes were billed for medication never given, routinely denied basic medical care as well as life saving procedures, and were found to have been beaten by staff members. Some say that Frank Bartrude got off too easy. The incident has sparked controversy over the lenient sentence for the white-collar criminal."

Susan looks up from her pillow and sits up in bed. "Kansas City, huh?"

CHAPTER 19:
TO AVENGE THE
HELPLESS

Susan stalks him, rolling along in her pickup truck as he exits a strip club, staggering down the streets of Kansas City. A man who never has laid a hand on anyone, but a man who kept his clean, while the hands of others spilled the blood of dozens of the helpless. A man who counted cash, sitting high up in his office, profiting off the pain, the suffering, and the deaths of the weak. A man who grew fat while he let others waste away. He steps aside into an alleyway, vomiting onto the pavement. She exits her truck, holding her broadsword in her right hand. Frank Bartrude looks at her with terror.

"Oh, God! Not you! From the fucking news! Listen, I've got cash, I can give you anything! Please don't!" he cries.

"You are irredeemable. You are sick. You are not worthy of your freedom," she tells him. She holds her sword in two hands, and she guts him like a fish. She grasps a can of black spray paint and stains her message into the wall of the alleyway:

CALL ME THE WOMAN

Made in the USA
Las Vegas, NV
22 June 2023

73746929R00049